I0811382

ESSENTIAL PETS

DOGS

BY CARLA MOONEY

Essential Library

An Imprint of Abdo Publishing

abdobooks.com

ABDOBOOKS.COM
Published by Abdo Publishing, a division of ABDO, PO Box 398166, Minneapolis, Minnesota 55439. Copyright © 2024 by Abdo Consulting Group, Inc. International copyrights reserved in all countries. No part of this book may be reproduced in any form without written permission from the publisher. Essential Library™ is a trademark and logo of Abdo Publishing.

Printed in the United States of America, North Mankato, Minnesota.
052023
092023

THIS BOOK CONTAINS RECYCLED MATERIALS

Cover Photos: Irina Oxilixo Danilova/Shutterstock Images (front and back)
Interior Photos: Alexia Khruscheva/Shutterstock Images, 1; Shutterstock Images, 3, 12–13, 16, 42–43, 45, 50, 54, 62–63, 68, 71, 84 (top), 84 (bottom), 92, 98, 101; Eric Isselee/Shutterstock Images, 4–5, 100; Jimartin Fotografo/Shutterstock Images, 7; Best Animal Photos/Shutterstock Images, 11; The Picture Art Collection/Alamy, 17; Csanad Kiss/Shutterstock Images, 19; Peter Lang/Shutterstock Images, 22–23; Iurii Osadchi/Shutterstock Images, 24; Christine Bird/Shutterstock Images, 27; Joana Toro/VIEWPress/Corbis News/Getty Images, 30; David Crane/MediaNews Group/Los Angeles Daily News/Getty Images, 32; Soloviova Liudmyla/Shutterstock Images, 36; Javier Brosch/Shutterstock Images, 38; Ingrid Pakats/Shutterstock Images, 48; Stephanie Keith/Getty Images News/Getty Images, 56; Zuzanna Paluch/Shutterstock Images, 59; Jorge Lemus/NurPhoto/Getty Images, 61; fotografixx/E+/Getty Images, 65; Mohssen Assanimoghaddam/picture alliance/Getty Images, 69; MShieldsPhotos/Alamy, 74; Vera Reva/Shutterstock Images, 78; Madelein Wolfaardt/Shutterstock Images, 81; Brandon Bell/Getty Images News/Getty Images, 82; Paul Chinn/San Francisco Chronicle/Hearst Newspapers/Getty Images, 88; Monkey Business Images/Shutterstock Images, 95; Ann Lillie/Shutterstock Images, 96; Beatriz Vera/Shutterstock Images, 97

Editor: Marie Pearson
Series Designer: Becky Daum

Library of Congress Control Number: 2022948869

PUBLISHER'S CATALOGING-IN-PUBLICATION DATA
Names: Mooney, Carla, author.
Title: Dogs / by Carla Mooney
Description: Minneapolis, Minnesota: Abdo Publishing Company, 2024 | Series: Essential pets | Includes online resources and index.
Identifiers: ISBN 9781098290535 (lib. bdg.) | ISBN 9781098276713 (ebook)
Subjects: LCSH: Pets--Juvenile literature. | Domestic dog--Juvenile literature. | Dogs --Juvenile literature. | Pets--Behavior--Juvenile literature. | Zoology--Juvenile literature.
Classification: DDC 636.0887--dc23

CONTENTS

CHAPTER 1

OUR BEST FRIEND

A small, furry form stretches on the bed as the sun peeks through the window blinds. In a split second, the sleepy dog sits up and intensely peers out the window. A low rumble starts in the dog's chest.

Sarah rolls over in bed and pats the blanket next to her. "Come over here, Lily," she says. "It's just someone walking outside." Lily turns away from the window and wiggles over to Sarah. Lily rolls on her back and cuddles in against Sarah's leg for a belly rub. Her tail starts wagging, and she licks Sarah's hand every time Sarah stops petting her. When Sarah sits up, the dog leaps off the bed, stands by the bedroom door, and looks expectantly at Sarah. It's time to go outside.

Many dogs will growl and bark as people or dogs walk near their home. These vocalizations can be in excitement or as a way to warn of possible trouble.

PLAYTIME

After going to the bathroom and coming back inside, the dog heads over to her toy basket in the living room. She noses through several stuffed toys and finds her current favorite, a stuffed chicken. Lily holds the chicken in her mouth and shakes it back and forth. Then she rolls onto her back and uses her paws to bat at the chicken. Sarah grabs another toy from the basket and tosses it to the other side of the room. Lily springs up, drops the chicken, and races to grab the second toy. She brings it back to Sarah, and they play this way for a while. The game is over when Lily returns to her chicken and takes it up on the chair to chew on it for a while. Then she settles in for a nap.

While the dog takes a quick nap, Sarah measures out her dog food and pours it into the food bowl. She fills the water bowl with fresh water. When Lily wakes up, she takes a few laps of water and nibbles at her food.

OBEDIENCE CLASSES

Regular training can help establish a routine with a dog and create a bond between dog and owner. Obedience classes are one way to get started with training a new dog. These training sessions teach owners how to teach their dogs good behavior and make it easier for the dogs to become happy and healthy family members. Dogs love structure and predictability, so early obedience training can give a new dog a great start.

Sarah heads to her home office for the next few hours to work. After eating, Lily joins her and dozes in a dog bed on the floor next to Sarah's desk, periodically checking to ensure her favorite human is still nearby. It is a familiar routine the two have perfected.

EXPLORING OUTSIDE

Later, Sarah turns to the dog. "Ready for a walk?" she asks. As the word "walk" comes out of Sarah's mouth, Lily's tail

Dogs need daily exercise. Walking helps dogs burn off some energy, and it can also keep them from getting bored, as sniffing and seeing new things helps engage their minds.

starts wagging. She runs to the pantry, where her leash is kept. Once Lily is geared up, they head out the door.

As they walk through the neighborhood, Lily trots along happily. She stops to sniff many times, especially at trees and posts that other dogs have recently visited. Along the way, Sarah and Lily spot another dog and its owner. Sarah reaches into her pocket for some treats and uses them to keep Lily's focus on her as the other dog passes them. After the walk, Sarah and Lily return home, and the dog heads to her water bowl for a long drink. Then it's time for another nap.

SMELL: A DOG'S SUPERIOR SENSE

A dog's sense of smell is so powerful it can detect the scent of a single drop of liquid in 20 Olympic-sized swimming pools. This impressive sensitivity is because of dog biology. The dog's nose has up to 300 million olfactory receptors, which receive smell information and send it to the brain for processing. Humans have approximately six million olfactory receptors. Dogs also have neophilia, which is an attraction to new and interesting smells.[1] Because a dog's sense of smell is so strong, it's a primary way a dog explores its world. This is why it's important to let dogs sniff on walks and in new places.

In the late afternoon, Lily and Sarah go outside in the backyard. Lily runs through the grass, sniffing different spots. Suddenly, she picks up a scent and follows it to the flower bed. She circles a large rock, sniffing at different sides and trying to push her nose underneath it. Dirt flies in the air as the dog digs in the bed, intently trying to reach something she has tracked to the rock. She works at it diligently for several minutes but comes up with nothing.

KEEPING CLEAN

When they come inside, Sarah wipes Lily's paws with a soft towel to clean off any dirt. Sometimes, Lily gets so dirty digging in the garden that Sarah has to take her immediately to the tub for a bath. This time, however, only the dog's paws need cleaning.

Next, it's time for brushing. Sarah sits on the floor with Lily and sprays her coat with a light detangling conditioner for dogs and then slowly brushes her tan-and-white hair. Lily is a Havanese. This breed does not shed hair regularly like some dog breeds, but her coat requires regular grooming and haircuts. Sarah tries to brush and comb the dog every day to keep Lily's hair from getting matted between trips to the groomer. Lily sits patiently as Sarah then gently combs her back, belly, legs, and tail. She saves the dog's head and ears for last. Once Lily is silky smooth, Sarah gives her one of her favorite meaty treats.

That night, as Sarah climbs into bed, Lily leaps onto the blanket to join her. Both are tired after a busy day, and Sarah reaches out and strokes Lily's back. It's been a good day.

MOST POPULAR PET

Worldwide, dogs are one of the most common pets. In the United States, more people own dogs than any other type of pet, with 69 million households having at least one dog, according to the 2021–2022 Pet Ownership Survey.[2] Often described as man's best friend, these four-legged creatures have provided friendship and companionship to people for thousands of years.

Dogs come in a variety of shapes and sizes but are all part of the same species, *Canis lupus familiaris*. One of the biggest dogs is the mastiff, which can weigh up to 230 pounds (104 kg).[3] Another is the Irish wolfhound, which can stand more than 30 inches (76 cm) tall at the shoulder.[4] In contrast, the tiny Chihuahua stands only five to eight inches (13–20 cm) tall and weighs six pounds (3 kg) or less.[5]

Some dogs have long, silky hair, while

DOG PROOFING FOR SAFETY

Dogs are like young children. They can get into things they shouldn't that can hurt them or make them sick. Responsible dog owners should dog proof their homes to keep their dogs safe and out of trouble. Childproof locks can secure cabinets with cleaning supplies or other hazardous materials. Houseplants should be moved off the floor to higher shelves or tables so the dog doesn't eat the leaves or dig in the dirt. People should secure garbage cans so that a dog cannot get into them. People should also use gates or close doors to block access to rooms that are off-limits to a curious dog.

Dogs have the most physical diversity of any land animal.

others have short, bristly hair, and some are even hairless. They can be black, brown, white, spotted, or striped. Their personalities can be as varied as their appearances. Some dogs are filled with endless energy, while others are happy to nap on the couch for most of the day.

One of the reasons why dogs are such popular pets is the connection these animals have with their owners. When people take the time to care for their dogs, providing for their physical needs along with giving them regular enrichment and training, many dogs return the favor with love and loyalty. Owners value the special bonds they form with their dogs.

CHAPTER 2

NATURAL HISTORY OF DOGS

The dog was the first animal to be domesticated. Early humans made an unusual partner, the wolf, thousands of years ago. Since then, the stories of humans and wolves have been linked together. And the wolves evolved in body and temperament. They became more submissive and less frightening, and their bodies changed, with some getting spots, curly tails, or floppy ears. The wolves became dogs.

EVOLUTION OF THE DOG

All of today's dog breeds descended from a species of wolf. DNA evidence suggests that modern dogs are descended from a species of Eurasian wolf.

Gray wolves and dogs descended from the same now-extinct ancient wolf species.

Researchers are working to determine which wolf species evolved into the dog.

Scientists believe dogs began to evolve from their wild wolf ancestors between 30,000 and 15,000 years ago. The domestication process likely happened gradually as the wolves became more used to being around humans. Some scientists believe that early humans actively tamed and bred wolves to help them with hunting. Others think it may have happened accidentally as wolves scavenged scraps of human food and gradually became comfortable staying close to human camps.

"Those wolves that were tamer and less aggressive would have been more successful at this. . . . While the humans did not initially gain any kind of benefit from this process, over time, they would have developed some kind of symbiotic relationship with these animals, eventually evolving into the dogs we see today," says Krishna Veeramah, a researcher from Stony Brook University.[1] With each generation, the wolves became tamer and more comfortable with humans. Eventually, over thousands of years, the wolves and humans became companions.

The earliest evidence of the connection between dogs and humans dates back to approximately 14,000 years ago. In 1914, scientists uncovered a grave in Oberkassel, Germany, that held the remains of a man, a woman, and a dog, along with several decorated objects. It is the earliest known grave where humans and dogs were buried together. According to scientists, the remains showed evidence of the humans caring for the dog when it was sick. "The evidence suggests this dog must have been special to somebody, and that these kinds of emotional relationships existed 14,000 years ago," says Keith Dobney, an archaeologist at the University of Liverpool.[2]

Scientists estimate that dogs began traveling alongside groups of humans approximately 20,000 years ago. By 7,000 years ago, dogs were common in human camps. However, they were not like today's pets. "They would likely have resembled dogs we today call village dogs," says Veeramah.[3] People do not control the breeding of these street dogs, which look similar around the world.

Evidence of the dog's place in human society can be found as far back as 3000 BCE. Illustrations of dogs have been uncovered on walls, tombs, and scrolls in Europe, the Middle East, and North America. Often the images show

ANCIENT EGYPT

Some of the earliest dog collars originated in ancient Egypt as simple rope leads. Over time, the collars evolved into thick leather rings that were joined with glue and pulled over the dog's head. Later, collars became even more intricate and decorated with copper and bronze studs. During the New Kingdom era (1570–1069 BCE), the ancient Egyptians inscribed gold and silver collars with their dogs' names. Leashes were attached to the collars and were typically made from leather or papyrus rope.

Village dogs are generally medium-sized dogs with narrow bodies, pricked ears, and short coats. In warm climates, they tend to be red in color.

dogs hunting game with their human partners. In other places, statues of dogs stand guard at the entrances of tombs. These relics show the importance dogs have held in human society for centuries.

BREEDING FOR JOBS

Humans began to breed dogs for desirable physical and behavioral traits. At first, humans selectively bred dogs for characteristics to make them better hunting companions or camp protectors. Humans migrated to different regions, and their dogs traveled with them. As dogs and humans spread into different climates and areas, new traits became desirable. This led to breeding for more characteristics specific to a place and way of life. This breeding eventually led to the hundreds of dog breeds and varieties seen in modern dogs.

For example, around 4,000 years ago, people in northeastern Asia used dogs for hunting and sledding. In the Siberian Arctic, they bred dogs to have thick coats to provide warmth in the cold climate. They also bred dogs to have the endurance to pull light loads over vast frozen ground and the temperament to work in packs as part of a sled team. Some of these dogs became the modern Siberian husky.

In ancient Greece, the giant Molossus dog was used as a guard to protect villages, people, children, and animals from enemies and predators. This immense dog was bred for traits that would help it perform as a guard dog. These dogs had thick, powerful bodies with loose skin that protected the head and neck. The Molossus's black brindle coloring made it intimidating in the daylight and

Alexander the Great bred Molossus dogs to fight in battle.

nearly impossible to see at night. Humans cropped the dog's floppy ears to improve hearing for guard duties. The ancient Molossus was crossbred with other dogs over the years, creating breeds such as the mastiff and Neapolitan mastiff.

In Germany, people bred dachshunds as hunting dogs, and these small dogs were sent after badgers. Their short legs kept them close to the ground to better track scents, while their long, narrow bodies helped them dig and crawl into badger burrows. Their floppy ears kept dirt and debris out of their ear canals. These small dogs have brave and fierce personalities to face badgers.

The Labrador retriever was originally bred by hunters in Newfoundland, Canada, and used to collect ducks and other game. The Lab's short, dense coat protects the dog from cold temperatures. Even more breeds were developed to protect homes, catch mice and vermin, and meet other needs.

While many dogs were bred for use in work and war, more recently, humans started breeding other types of dogs to make them better companions. For example, the French bulldog originated in England in the late 1700s when the bulldog was paired with smaller dogs to breed a smaller, more docile version of the bulldog. The little Frenchie is playful, alert, and adaptable, all qualities that make it a desirable companion.

DOG SPOTLIGHT

SAINT BERNARD

The exact origin of the Saint Bernard dog is unknown, but its ancestors were likely mastiffs that traveled from Rome to Switzerland during times of war. Around 1700 CE, the dogs began to work with monks at the Great Saint Bernard Hospice and Monastery during the frigid winter months. The dogs joined the monks on patrols and rescue missions to help people stranded on Swiss mountains during snowstorms.

The monks trained and bred the dogs to find and rescue travelers buried by avalanches. Male dogs were trained to dig through the snow to find people and lie on top of fallen people to give them warmth in the freezing cold.

Today's Saint Bernards stand between 26 and 30 inches (66–76 cm) at the shoulder and weigh between 120 and 180 pounds (54–82 kg), with males generally larger than females.[4] With training, they are gentle and good with children. As with all large dogs, training must start when they are very young so that they do not accidentally hurt someone by jumping on people or pulling on a leash.

MODERN DOGS

Today, dogs come in many shapes and sizes. The Fédération Cynologique Internationale recognized 356 breeds of dogs in 2022.[5] Many other dogs are mixed breeds, a blend of two or more breeds.

Today, some dogs still work as hunting, herding, or military dogs. Military working dogs assist soldiers with tracking and patrols, while dogs that work with law enforcement sniff out drugs and explosives. And more recently, some have taken new jobs as service dogs, working as guides and assistants, performing daily tasks to help their owners with disabilities. Others are therapy dogs, bringing joy and comfort to many people. Talented acting dogs entertain the world on stages and screens. However, most modern dogs' main job is to provide companionship. These dogs still need to use their minds, so some owners train their dogs for competitions.

Most dog jobs require specific training and lots of practice. The assignments use and build on the traits and characteristics the dogs already possess. Often, dogs use their sharp senses—hearing, sight, and smell—at work. Some jobs can be difficult, and not every dog will succeed. Traits such as intelligence, obedience, good memory, willingness to learn, awareness and attention to surroundings, and concentration are essential factors for both training and performance on the job.

DESIGNER DOGS

Not everyone is a fan of designer dogs. In some cases, combining two breeds does not produce the desired traits. For example, a goldendoodle puppy may have a coat that is more like its golden retriever parent and sheds more than desired. Also, designer dogs can fetch a high price, which makes them attractive to puppy-mill breeders and unreliable sellers. These dogs can be at greater risk of health problems due to living conditions and because breeders may not be removing dogs with genetic diseases from their breeding stock.

Today, people can choose between a purebred dog or a mixed-breed dog. Purebreds are valued for their predictability. Breeders of purebred dogs generally breed for a certain look and temperament. Purebred dogs also generally fall into a predictable size range for the breed.

A mixed breed may have just two breeds, or it could have so many that even DNA tests can't determine all of them. Some mixed breeds result from the accidental mating of pets, and others come from feral street dogs. Others, sometimes nicknamed designer dogs, are purposely mixed from two or more breeds. Mixed breeds are generally less predictable in temperament and appearance. Littermates may have very different traits. Intentionally bred mixed-breed dogs have become popular alternatives to purebred dogs in recent years, and they include the goldendoodle (a golden retriever and poodle mix), Shichon (a bichon frise and Shih Tzu mix), and Bernedoodle (a Bernese mountain dog and poodle mix).

CHAPTER 3

GETTING A NEW DOG

Dogs can live 15 years or longer and have a lot of physical and social needs, so getting a dog is a serious responsibility.[1] It takes a lot of research and preparation before the dog arrives home. Putting in the work from the beginning can help a new dog and its human family start their lives together in the best way possible.

CHOOSING THE RIGHT DOG

Every dog is different, and every human family is different. A dog that does not fit well into one family may be the perfect addition to another family. One essential step in getting a new dog is knowing what qualities will make a dog most compatible with a family and home. Choosing the right dog breed can greatly affect how smoothly a dog fits into a family.

Puppies are cute, but they are a lot of work. People should consider whether they can commit to the time it will take to raise them.

Many breeds were developed for jobs that involved a lot of daily running, so they often need a lot of exercise as pets.

Prospective dog owners should consider several factors when deciding what type of dog to get. First, the size of a person's home is an important factor when picking a dog. People may live in apartments that have size restrictions on dogs. They may need to look for a dog that will be under a certain weight as an adult. People in an apartment may also find that a large dog would take up too much space in their home.

The dog's activity level should also be considered. A high-energy dog may not have enough space to live comfortably in an apartment, while a lower-energy dog may thrive in the limited space with regular walks.

However, the family's activity level also influences the choice. A high-energy dog may be fine in an apartment with a very active person who will jog with the dog daily. And just because someone has a yard doesn't mean a high-energy dog will be a good fit. Many dogs become bored if they are given only their yard to sniff around, so a homeowner with a yard may need a low-energy dog if that person will not walk the dog frequently. Potential owners should assess their lifestyle to determine what type of dog would fit best into their activities. Finding a dog that matches its owner's activity level will make everyone happiest.

Another factor in choosing the right dog is the family schedule. Will someone be home with the dog most of the day, or will the family spend much time at work or traveling? Some breeds are more independent and do not mind being left alone during the day, while other dogs can be unhappy spending hours alone. Each dog breed also has typical personality traits. Some breeds may prefer some time to themselves, while others constantly follow their owners from room to room.

Potential owners can research different breeds to determine which ones are most compatible with their lifestyles. "Consider first if you are looking for an affectionate companion, an energetic running buddy, an aloof roommate [or] a playmate for the kids.

Knowing what you would like to achieve in this relationship with your new pet will help you make the best choice when deciding which pet is best suited for your family," says Jodi Andersen, a dog trainer and cofounder of How I Met My Dog, a company that matches people with adoptable dogs.[2]

Other qualities are also important when choosing a dog, such as whether anyone in the family is allergic to dogs. A hypoallergenic breed such as the poodle might be a good fit. Hypoallergenic breeds are less likely to trigger allergies, although some people have allergic reactions to all dogs. It is best for a person with allergies to try to spend time with several dogs closely related to the one that may be purchased or do a trial period living with the dog the family wants to purchase.

SEPARATION ANXIETY

Some dogs experience separation anxiety when left alone at home. Common signs of separation anxiety include digging and scratching at doors or windows to reach the owner, destructive chewing, howling, barking, and whining. A house-trained dog may also have accidents in the house. Physical and mental stimulation can help a dog reduce its stress and anxiety. One strategy for dealing with separation anxiety is taking the dog for a walk in a new place before leaving. It can also help to give the dog a treat toy stuffed with treats or a food puzzle, where the dog has to figure out how to get treats, in order to occupy and distract it while its owners are gone. For more severe cases, medication may be necessary, and a veterinarian can help.

PUPPY OR ADULT DOG?

Once a potential owner researches a compatible dog breed, the next decision is whether to get a puppy or an adult dog. Throughout a dog's life, its personality and needs change. A puppy requires a lot of work, energy, and patience. The puppy phase can last up to two years, depending on the dog. During that time, owners will need to work on basic training, manners, and house-training. Puppies have accidents in the house and often get into things they shouldn't. One of the benefits of buying a puppy is that owners can bond with the dog early on and ensure that it receives proper training and

Puppies naturally bite and chew. Owners need to gently teach them the right things to chew.

socialization with dogs and humans. Owners can use this very impressionable time to teach the manners that are important to them and make sure behavior problems don't happen in the first place.

An adult dog may be a better choice if a potential owner does not have the time or energy to devote to training a new puppy. Adult dogs have established personalities and are often calmer than puppies. Many adult dogs already know basic commands and are house-trained. In some cases, adult dogs may not have received proper training or socialization, and they may have developed undesirable habits and behaviors. For example, some adult dogs may not be a good fit for a family with young children, who can be rough with dogs, because of a traumatic experience in their past that makes them more defensive around people.

THE RIGHT PLACE

There are many ways to find the right dog. Some people decide to buy a dog from a responsible dog breeder. Getting a dog from a responsible breeder may be the best choice for families with specific needs. By working with a reputable breeder, potential owners can be clear about the qualities they desire in a dog. Breeders have information about puppies' parents and lineage, so they have a good idea of dogs' adult size, temperament, and health. Responsible breeders will do genetic health tests for known issues in the breed to reduce the risk of illness in the puppies they breed. In addition, many breeders will evaluate the personalities of the puppies in a litter and help match a puppy to a family based on their evaluation.

However, getting a dog from a breeder can be expensive. It often costs more than $1,000 to get a dog from a responsible breeder.[3] And not all breeders are reputable. The American Kennel Club (AKC) and many breed clubs provide lists of questions owners can ask to determine if a breeder is responsible. But no matter how responsible a breeder is, no one can guarantee a puppy will have the desired traits as it grows into an adult dog.

Other people decide to adopt a puppy or adult dog from an animal shelter or

BREEDER RED FLAGS

Not every breeder is reputable. Responsible breeders often work only with one or two breeds and have only a few litters a year. They have at least one of the puppies' parents on-site, so prospective pet owners can meet the pups' close relatives. Responsible breeders also ensure a puppy is a good fit for a family, perform at least one complete physical exam, and provide veterinary contact information. Buyers should beware of potential red flags if the breeder always has puppies available, does not interview or meet a person before selling a puppy, and provides no evidence of veterinary care or genetic health testing.

Some rescues hold adoption events where potential buyers can meet many dogs available for adoption at once.

rescue organization. Shelters and rescues have dogs of all ages, including many adult dogs. Compared with buying a dog from a breeder, adopting a dog from a shelter or rescue can be much less expensive.

Many dogs in shelters and rescues are mixed breed and have unknown parentage. Shelter workers may have some information about a dog's mother but little about its genetic history. This lack of knowledge can make it difficult to predict temperament or how large a puppy will grow.

In addition, the dog may not be fully trained or socialized, or it may have even been abused or abandoned. These dogs can need additional care and training to help them overcome past traumas and adapt to their new homes, and sometimes they need lifelong management. Getting an adult dog that has been in a foster home for a while can give buyers the best insight into the dog's temperament and needs. Buyers should also screen shelters and rescues and try to determine if they are generally honest about the health and temperament of the dogs they sell.

BRINGING A NEW DOG HOME

Bringing a new dog home is exciting, but it can also be stressful for the dog and owner until everyone settles into a new routine. To make the transition as smooth as possible, owners should gather items the dog will need in advance, including a collar, an identification tag, a harness, a leash, food and water bowls, a dog bed, and toys. Some owners will also set up a crate or pet playpen to create a safe space for the dog or puppy. Owners should get a small bag of what the dog has been eating to keep its diet consistent during the transition to its new home.

Before the dog arrives, family members should also discuss the pet's routine and care responsibilities. They should plan regular walks and feeding times and decide where the dog will sleep and whether any areas of the house will be off-limits. If bringing home a puppy, they should be sure to puppy proof the house and remove any dangerous items that could harm the dog.

When possible, owners should plan for the dog to arrive at a time when they can spend a few days with it

A veterinary exam will help determine any special care a person's new dog may need.

to ease its transition into the household. Dog and owner should spend some time getting to know each other and establish a consistent routine. A routine will help the dog learn what to expect in its new home and develop trust with its owner. Transitioning to a new home can be overwhelming for a dog, so the owner should be sure to keep things quiet and consistent for the first week or two.

VISITING THE VET

Ideally, a veterinarian should examine a new dog within a week of its arrival. At this first visit, the vet will do a thorough examination to make sure the dog is healthy. The vet will review any medical records to learn about any pre-existing conditions. They will perform a physical exam and check the dog's eyes, ears, heart, lungs, and more. The exam helps the vet establish a baseline for the dog to help with future visits. Dr. Felicia Magnaterra, a veterinarian who works with shelter animals, says of initial exams, "This allows for the veterinarian to establish a relationship and baseline examination of the pet, which will help inform a monitoring schedule to ensure lifelong quality health care and disease prevention."[4]

The veterinarian will also talk about pet care and how to help the dog adjust to its new home. They may prescribe medications to prevent fleas, ticks, and heartworms and other internal parasites. The vet may also

CRATE TRAINING

Many dogs have the instinct to find a comfortable, quiet, and safe place when they feel overwhelmed. Crate training teaches a dog to view its crate as a safe, secure place where it can go. A dog's crate should be big enough for the dog to stand up and turn around. However, it should not be so large that the dog can use it to go to the bathroom. The crate should have a comfortable bed, though some dogs with thick or long fur may need a cooling pad. Pet owners can slowly introduce the dog to the crate by giving it treats and feeding it in the crate. Crate training can take days or weeks, depending on the dog.

recommend certain vaccinations to protect the dog from disease. The veterinarian may discuss socialization and training options.

The veterinarian will also discuss options with the owner if a dog has not been spayed or neutered. The decision to spay or neuter a dog is a complex issue. Spaying and neutering will prevent dogs from breeding. It reduces the risk of certain cancers and infections related to the reproductive system. However, it can also increase the risk of some joint issues and cancers such as lymphoma and osteosarcoma. Spaying a dog can cause as many as 20 percent of females to develop urinary incontinence.[5] Dog owners should carefully research and discuss this issue with a trusted veterinarian.

BONDING WITH A NEW DOG

The first weeks and months with a new dog can be an excellent opportunity to establish a strong bond. Bonding is different with every dog. Some dogs bond quickly with their new families, while others can take a few weeks or months. It is essential to be patient with the dog as it learns to trust the new people and surroundings in its life. Owners should plan to give a new dog time to adjust to its home and feel safe.

Several activities can help strengthen a bond with a dog. Training activities help a dog learn desired behaviors and deepen the connection between dog and human. During training, the dog focuses on its owner and earns praise, treats, and playtime, which builds its confidence. Exercising together, playing together, and grooming are other ways to establish and strengthen a bond with a dog. Other forms of physical contact, such as petting and cuddling, can also develop and strengthen a bond with a dog that enjoys those things.

Dogs thrive on routine. When a person creates a routine with a dog, the pet learns what to expect from its person and develops trust. Consistent routines also help a dog understand what is expected of it and become confident in making its person happy.

CHAPTER 4

TAKING CARE OF A DOG

Being a dog owner is a commitment that lasts for the dog's lifetime. A dog owner is responsible for ensuring the dog is happy and healthy. Taking care of a dog involves more than just putting food in a bowl or taking it for a walk. It involves many other responsibilities, including providing complete nutrition, monitoring its health, grooming, cleaning, training, exercising, playing, and more.

NUTRITION AND FOOD

One of the most critical choices a dog owner can make is what type of food to feed a dog. No matter the kind, owners should purchase foods that are labeled as meeting the Association of American Feed Control Officials (AAFCO) nutritional guidelines for being a complete, balanced diet.

Owners should play with their dogs to help strengthen their bond. Some dogs enjoy playing with toys, but others prefer playing chase or other games.

While most dogs do best eating set meals, they should have constant access to fresh water.

This will help ensure the dog is getting the nutrients it needs.

Dry kibble and canned wet dog food are the most popular food options. Dry food lasts a long time and does not need to be refrigerated. It is also easy to measure and is typically the cheapest option. Wet food also has a long storage life, but it can be expensive, and it can't be left sitting out for long before it spoils. However, it can be especially good for dogs that don't drink enough water or for dogs that have trouble chewing. Most dogs prefer the taste of wet food, and it can help them feel full longer since they need a greater volume of food, because water does not have much nutrients.

Some dog foods are semimoist. They have a bit less water than wet food. These foods are often shaped like burgers or other meat-like products. Many of these foods contain artificial flavors and colors. While they might be suitable for a treat, most veterinarians do not recommend a diet of semimoist foods.

Some dog owners buy fresh food for their pets, which includes gently cooked and raw foods. These can be purchased at stores or made at home. Some owners prefer fresh food because it requires fewer synthetic nutrients than other kinds of foods. Researchers remain uncertain of how well even the human body can use synthetic nutrients. Some people prefer fresh-food diets for their dogs because studies with humans have shown that processed foods are linked to an increased risk of cancer.

Home-cooked food allows an owner to completely control a dog's diet and ensure their pet is getting the right nutrition, using ingredients such as beef, chicken, salmon, and more. Fresh, natural food has many benefits for a dog's health and well-being, promotes heart health, and increases energy. However, preparing home-cooked meals for a dog can be time-consuming and expensive. If dog owners choose this diet, they should research dog nutrition to ensure their dog is getting all the nutrients it needs. Working with a veterinary nutritionist can ensure the dog is getting the right nutrients.

Some dog owners feed their dogs a raw diet. A raw diet is mainly raw meat, bones, and organs. Raw eggs, yogurt or other dairy products, and dog-safe fruits and vegetables are commonly added. As with home-cooked foods, a canine nutritionist should ensure the homemade raw diet is balanced. Those who prefer a raw-food diet say it gives their dog a shinier coat, healthier skin, better dental health, and increased energy. Great care must be taken with handling raw food, and many veterinarians recommend that puppies not be fed a raw-food diet. The American Veterinary Medical Association (AVMA) opposes the

HOW OFTEN DO DOGS EAT?

How often a dog should be fed depends on the dog's age. Generally, a dog's veterinarian can recommend a suitable feeding schedule. Typically, young puppies need to eat more frequently than adult dogs. Puppies between eight and 12 weeks old should eat four meals per day. Between three and six months, puppies need to eat three meals daily. Once the puppy reaches six months to one year, meals should drop to two per day. By the time a dog turns one year old, one meal daily is sufficient, but daily food can be split into two smaller meals.[1]

unregulated feeding of raw foods. The AVMA says raw foods that have not been properly processed may contain pathogens harmful to dogs and people.

EXERCISE AND PLAYTIME

Dogs need daily exercise to burn calories and stimulate their minds. Daily walks are an essential part of a dog's exercise routine. The frequency, length, and intensity of the walk depend on the dog. Some dogs are happy with a short walk, while others need longer walks to burn off excess energy. "For those dogs, it can be helpful to include games such as fetch in their daily routine, or other activities such as agility, dock diving, or nose work," says Zazie Todd, a certified dog trainer.[2]

Using a well-fitting collar or harness and leash when walking a dog outside is important. This keeps a dog safe and under control. A leash also keeps a dog from unexpectedly darting into traffic or chasing prey.

Many dogs also enjoy off-leash exercise in a secure and safe place. "It's really good for dogs to get some off-leash time, both for the exercise and because it gives them the opportunity to choose what they're doing for a while," says Todd.[3] Off-leash activity can occur in a fenced-in backyard, a local dog park, a hiking trail, or other suitable places. When off-leash, a dog should be trained to follow cues and return to its owner's side when called. If a dog

Some beaches allow off-leash dogs and can be great spots for well-trained dogs to run and play.

can't be trusted off-leash, a long line can sometimes be used, but owners should check local laws to make sure they aren't breaking any leash rules.

Playtime is another way for dogs to exercise. It also stimulates their minds and helps prevent boredom, which can lead to destructive behaviors. "Dogs are companion animals, so it's good for their mental well-being to have positive interaction with their human," says Dr. Jim Carlson, owner of an animal clinic and hospital in the suburbs of Chicago.[4] Some dogs enjoy playing a game of fetch, others prefer tug-of-war, and some like to play chase with their people or be chased. Many playtime

games satisfy a dog's instincts to dig, herd, chew, chase, and fetch.

GROOMING

To maintain health, dogs need regular grooming. Some people groom their dogs themselves, while others take them to a professional groomer. Some dogs have very few grooming needs. Others take a lot of work. All dogs need their nails trimmed regularly. "Overgrown nails can create problems throughout the body, especially in the back and hips. When I see a pet come in with pain symptoms, the feet are the first place I look," says Dr. Carlson.

Some people trim their dogs' nails themselves, while others have a groomer or veterinarian cut them.[5]

A dog's coat needs regular brushing. Brushing helps spread oils through the fur, keeping it healthy and shiny. Brushing also removes dead hair and potential allergens. Dogs with long hair should be brushed and combed several times a week to help prevent the dog's hair from getting matted.

A NEED TO CHEW

Most dogs are born with a need to chew. It is one way they explore their world. For puppies, chewing relieves pain when teething. Older dogs chew to keep their teeth clean and their jaws strong. Other dogs chew because it's fun. Dogs also chew to relieve stress, anxiety, frustration, and boredom. To keep a dog from chewing a pair of shoes or a piece of furniture, pet owners should provide their dogs with appropriate chew toys and edible chews.

How often a dog needs a bath depends on the breed, coat, and activities. Some dogs need baths and haircuts every six to eight weeks. Others need a bath only if they get dirty or smelly. Baths with dog-specific shampoos and conditioners will help keep their coats healthy and shiny.

REGULAR VETERINARY CARE

Just like humans, dogs need regular medical checkups to ensure they stay healthy. Regular vet visits can prevent disease and allow vets to detect and treat problems early.

At an annual visit, a veterinarian can detect health issues such as heart problems, allergies, ear or eye infections, arthritis, obesity, dental problems, gastrointestinal problems, and other issues.

Most healthy dogs should visit their veterinarian annually for a complete exam. Puppies and senior dogs may need to see the vet more frequently. At an annual

Dogs that need haircuts will be more expensive to groom professionally. If groomed at home, the owner will need to purchase more grooming tools than for a dog that does not need haircuts.

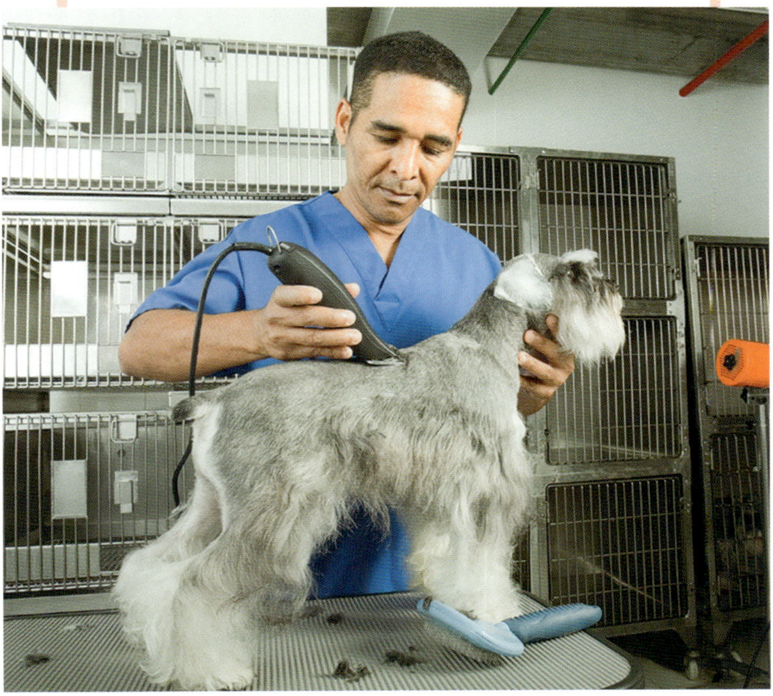

MICROCHIPPING

According to the AKC, one in three pets gets lost at some point in its lifetime. Collars and identification tags can fall off, making it nearly impossible to reunite the pet with its family. The most effective way to get a lost pet back to its owner is to insert a microchip under its skin. A microchip is approximately the size of a grain of rice and is inserted with a needle under the skin between a dog's shoulder blades. The microchip is registered, and the owner's contact information is entered. When scanned, the microchip transmits a unique ID number that identifies the dog and its owner's contact information.

visit, veterinarians can administer routine vaccinations and perform diagnostic tests such as blood tests for heartworms and fecal tests for parasites. Standard vaccinations include rabies, distemper, parvovirus, Bordetella, and canine influenza.

Dental health is an integral part of a dog's health. A veterinarian will examine the dog's mouth and teeth to assess oral health. At least 80 percent of dogs older than three years have periodontal disease.[6] This disease can destroy gum tissue and bone, leading to tooth loss. Tissue and bone bacterial infections can also spread and put a dog at risk of other more severe complications.

To keep a dog's teeth healthy, owners can regularly brush the dog's teeth at home using a toothpaste designed for dogs. A veterinarian can also perform an annual dental cleaning in which the dog is placed under general anesthesia for the cleaning. The vet can check for other issues, such as oral masses or tooth fractures, during the cleaning. Between brushings, dog dental chews can also help keep a dog's teeth healthy.

PEST AND PARASITE PROTECTION

Fleas and ticks are some of the most common pests that can cause canine health problems. Fleas can cause itching, hair loss, allergic reactions, skin infections, tapeworms, and anemia. Ticks can lead to even more severe health problems and spread bacterial and protozoal diseases such as Lyme disease and Rocky Mountain spotted fever. These diseases can make a dog very sick if not diagnosed and treated.

There are several options to protect a dog from fleas and ticks. Many products, such as collars, shampoos, sprays, and topical medications, can be purchased at a pet store. Veterinarians can also prescribe flea and tick medications.

Heartworm disease is another serious disease that can affect dogs. Heartworms are parasites spread by mosquitos. When a mosquito carrying heartworm larvae bites a dog, the heartworms travel through the dog's bloodstream to the heart and to blood vessels in the lungs. As the worms grow, they can cause significant damage to those vessels and organs. A veterinarian

Teaching a dog to walk at a person's side can help the dog with loose-leash walking.

will test a dog annually for heartworms and prescribe medication that dogs should take to protect against the disease.

TRAINING

For responsible dog owners, training never ends. It begins when a dog first comes home and continues throughout its lifetime. "Dogs don't come already knowing how we would like them to behave, so we need to train them so they know what to do," says Todd.[7]

Obedience training teaches a dog good manners. It also introduces the dog to behaviors necessary for keeping it healthy and safe. For example, teaching a dog to come when called can stop it from running into traffic. Training can also help a dog cope with scary situations like going to the vet or being home alone.

Training stimulates a dog both physically and mentally. Training that uses positive reinforcement is a fun way to engage a dog. Positive reinforcement training uses praise, treats, or toys when a dog performs the desired behavior. Daily training throughout a dog's lifetime creates and reinforces desired behaviors and strengthens the bond between a dog and its owner.

Regular care keeps a dog happy and healthy. It can also prevent many problems in the future. Routine veterinary visits, proper food and nutrition, adequate exercise and playtime, and ongoing training are all essential to keep a dog thriving throughout its lifetime.

CHAPTER 5

INDUSTRY AND COMMUNITY

Dogs are big business around the world. The pet industry generates billions of dollars annually, providing products and services for pets, including dogs. The community of dogs and dog lovers extends further, from local dog groups and rescues to national agility competitions and international dog shows. All around the world, dogs are making their mark.

THE COST OF DOGS

Caught up in the excitement of bringing home a new dog, many people do not consider the financial commitment owning a dog brings. The reality is that owning a dog involves recurring costs for the dog's lifetime. The cost of owning a dog varies by breed, location, and health of the individual dog. In the first year, most dog owners spend between $405 and $2,200

There are many expenses to dog ownership. Some, such as food, must be purchased often. Others, such as harnesses, usually only need to be bought to replace damaged ones.

PET INSURANCE

No one plans for their dog to get sick. Illnesses and injuries occur, and vet bills can add up quickly. To protect against unplanned vet bills, some dog owners purchase pet insurance. Just like human health insurance, pet insurance is a health-care policy that reimburses an owner for some unexpected costs when a dog has an emergency or severe illness.

on their dogs, according to a 2022 analysis by *Canine Journal*. Expenses in the first year include purchase fees, routine vet fees, heartworm prevention, flea and tick medication, collars, ID tags, leashes, food, bowls, treats, toys, bedding, and crates. After the first year, annual costs drop slightly to $326 to $1,982.[1]

There are also some additional costs to consider when owning a dog. Extra services such as pet sitting, training, and professional grooming are other expenses that pet owners incur from time to time. Emergency vet services may also be needed if the dog becomes ill or gets injured.

A BILLION-DOLLAR INDUSTRY

The pet industry is a major force in the United States and worldwide. In 2021, annual pet industry revenue reached more than $126 billion in the United States and included live animal purchases, pet food, pet supplies, pet services, and vet care. The highest-selling product category was pet food, with sales of approximately $50 billion in 2021.[2] Within the pet food category, dry dog food was the biggest seller. Four companies dominate the dog food category in the United States. These are Mars Petcare, Nestlé Purina Petcare, Hill's Pet Nutrition, and Spectrum Brands. These four companies produce most of the well-known dog food brands, including Pedigree, Purina Pro Plan, Hill's Science Diet, and Iams.

After pet food, vet care and over-the-counter medicine and pet supplies were the second- and third-largest contributors, respectively, to pet industry revenues in 2021.[3] Two companies in the United States dominate the pet store market: PetSmart and Petco. These two companies captured more than 40 percent of the pet store market in 2022.[4] These stores sell most things pet owners need, such as food, treats, grooming supplies, bedding, training tools, toys, and more. They also offer grooming services, in-store and online training, and veterinary services within many stores. There are also locally owned pet stores throughout the United States. These tend to have high-quality products and staff who are educated about the products they sell, so they can be helpful in answering questions.

BUILDING A COMMUNITY

Nationwide, communities of dog lovers have formed to support dogs and their owners. In local neighborhoods, dog parks provide a way to meet nearby dog lovers.

People bring their dogs to the park for exercise and canine playtime, while the owners can chat with other dog owners. At the dog park, owners can form bonds and share information about veterinarians, groomers, pet stores, and different dog-related needs.

Many people take training classes at local centers. They may take classes to help train manners. They might start training to help solve behavior issues. Or they may train their dogs as something fun to do and to keep their

Some dogs have expenses others won't have. Shorthaired dogs that live in places that get cold may need sweaters.

dogs from getting bored. Many people meet fellow dog lovers at these classes.

There are also more formalized dog communities. Founded in 1884, the AKC is a not-for-profit organization that provides education about dog breeds, canine health, and training. The AKC is also the largest registry for purebred dogs in the United States. It offers several registration options. If a dog is registered as a purebred, that means the dog, its parents, and its ancestors are all of one breed and have been registered for generations. The AKC also offers registration for spayed and neutered mixed breeds or purebreds of unregistered parents so they can compete in some sports.

According to its website, the AKC says, "We encourage dogs as family companions; advance canine health and well-being; advocate for dog owner rights; and educate the public about responsible dog ownership. We are passionate about everything related to dogs, and we celebrate the joy they bring to our lives every single day."[5] In addition to maintaining its registry of purebred dogs, the AKC promotes and sanctions numerous events for dogs across the nation. Another national dog organization is the United Kennel Club (UKC), which also maintains a dog registry and sponsors competitions.

There are breed-specific dog clubs across the United States too. Many national breed clubs have local chapters

One of the most famous AKC dog shows is the Westminster Kennel Club Dog Show, which has been held since 1877, making it the second-longest continuously running sporting event in the United States.

where dog owners can meet other dog lovers who are passionate about a specific dog breed. Breed clubs provide education, training, and care designed for a particular breed. "Connecting with my local groups has allowed me to find local resources when moving to a new place. That includes competent vets, dog walkers, sitters, dog-friendly businesses, and new friends. It's also helped tremendously when dealing with quirky breed health and wellness issues," says Erin Mulrooney, who has a greyhound.[6] These clubs also sponsor breed-specific events and training sessions. They organize fun outings and events for dogs and owners.

CONFORMATION

Some purebred dogs compete in a type of dog show called conformation. In a conformation show, dogs are judged on how closely they match, or conform to, their breed's standard, which is a written description of how the breed should look and behave. The closer a dog's appearance matches the breed's standard, the more likely the dog will produce puppies that also meet the breed standard.

Some conformation shows are large and feature many breeds. Other times, clubs will host a show with a single breed. During the show, each dog is shown by its owner or a handler. Some owners take their dogs to a conformation class that teaches dog and owner what to do at the events. Competing dogs should be well groomed, be comfortable around other dogs, and know basic manners, such as walking on a leash and being comfortable in a crate.

DOG SPORTS

Sports can be fun for both the dog and the owner. Sports provide a lot of mental and physical stimulation for a dog.

For breeds that need significant exercise, sports are a great way to burn off excess energy. Every year, there are thousands of sports events. Most allow dogs of all breeds and mixes. People pay to enter the competitions. Many also pay to enter classes to train for competitions. Registries such as the AKC and UKC sponsor many sports events.

Agility is one of the most popular dog activities in the United States. Agility tests a dog's physical and mental abilities. In an agility competition, a dog navigates through an obstacle course that includes various walkways, jumps, tunnels, weave poles, and more. The obstacles must be completed in order and as fast as possible, and the dog that completes all obstacles correctly in the fastest time wins. Several clubs and organizations have formed specifically for agility sports, including the United States Dog Agility Association

TRICK DOG COMPETITION

Some dogs compete in trick dog events. The dog learns a short routine four to six minutes long composed of unique tricks that can include props, music, and costumes. In 2021, a miniature poodle named Eli won the 2021 national AKC Virtual Trick Dog Competition. In his Batman superhero routine, Eli performed 31 tricks in six minutes, moving through a comic-book scene to defeat the Riddler.[7] Owner Leslie Gelesh spent four months creating the trick routine and building a set to display Eli's talents in their "Batman Furever" routine.

One of the most challenging agility obstacles to teach a dog to complete is the weave poles.

and the North American Dog Agility Council. The AKC and UKC also have agility competitions.

Flyball is another popular dog sport, especially for fast, high-energy dogs. In a flyball competition, teams of four dogs compete in a relay race, running down a series of hurdles, retrieving a ball from a flyball box, and then returning the ball to the start, where the next dog takes its turn. The team that finishes in the fastest time wins.

Obedience competitions have been part of dog sports for nearly 100 years. Judges rate the dogs on their ability to obey commands, from basic to complicated. Commands include heelwork, sit-and-stays, and retrieving.

DOCK DIVING

Dock diving is a sport for dogs that love leaping into the water. Dogs of all breeds and sizes can participate as long as they know how to swim. Owners toss a toy into the water, and dogs take a running leap from a long dock after it. The dogs are judged by the distance of their jump. In other variations of dock diving, dogs compete for the highest jump or the fastest retrieval.

Some competitions test a dog's sense of smell. Dogs use their noses to find hidden cotton swabs dipped in one of four essential oils. When a dog finds one, it alerts its owner, such as by sitting.

DOG RESCUE GROUPS

Thousands of dog rescue groups and animal shelters throughout the country work tirelessly to help dogs find loving homes. Shelters are often run and funded by local governments, while rescue groups are usually nonprofits funded by donations and adoption fees. Many of the people who keep them running are volunteers. Some dog rescues are breed specific, while others work with all types of dogs.

Rescue groups and shelters take in dogs that have been abandoned, abused, or neglected. Many shelters house the dogs on-site in kennels. A rescue will often use volunteers to foster dogs in their homes until a suitable permanent family can be found. While a dog is in their care, these groups provide veterinary care, training, and playing. They also begin dealing with behavior issues.

Shelters and rescues are the most common places for people to get a dog. Between 2021 and 2022, 39 percent of people acquiring a new dog got one from a shelter or rescue. In that same time, just 29 percent got a dog from a breeder or pet store.[8]

Some rescues focus on greyhounds that are looking for new homes after retiring from racing.

CHAPTER 6

LAWS AND REGULATIONS

Dog owners in the United States are responsible for knowing and following laws and regulations related to their pets. There are few federal laws regarding dogs. The Animal Welfare Act regulates dogs bred and sold commercially. The Preventing Animal Cruelty and Torture Act makes torture of dogs and other small animals illegal. But most laws relating to dogs are state or local laws that vary from place to place. Most areas have laws or regulations regarding vaccinations, pet waste and disposal, licensing, leash requirements, and dog bites and injuries from dogs.

VACCINATION REQUIREMENTS

Most cities and states require that all dogs are vaccinated against rabies. Rabies is a viral disease

Many cities require a dog to be up-to-date on its rabies vaccine before an owner can get a license.

that spreads through the bite of an infected animal. The rabies virus affects the central nervous system and, if untreated, can cause death. Most rabies cases occur in wild animals such as bats, raccoons, skunks, and foxes. However, any mammal, including dogs and humans, can get rabies.

If an infected animal bites a dog, the dog can also become infected. And if the dog bites a human, the human can get rabies. Laws requiring rabies vaccination for all dogs are in place to protect the human population. How often dogs need to get rabies booster shots can vary by state and city. In addition, some areas require the vaccination to be administered by a licensed veterinary professional, while others allow owners to vaccinate their dogs. In a few cases, a state may grant an exemption from the vaccination requirement if a veterinarian determines the vaccine may be a medical risk to the dog. Owners who fail to vaccinate their dogs for rabies can be fined or even given jail time. In some cases, they may lose possession of their dogs.

While other vaccinations may not be required by state or local law, they may be required by other organizations. For example, boarding and grooming facilities often require dogs to have several vaccinations before allowing them on the premises. Commonly required vaccinations include vaccines for distemper, parvovirus, Bordetella, and

The rabies vaccine is typically given in a muscle, such as the large muscles near the hip.

canine influenza. These requirements are necessary to protect the health of other dogs and employees.

DISPOSAL OF PET WASTE

Many cities and local communities have ordinances that require dog owners to pick up and properly dispose of pet waste when not on their property. Dog feces is an

POOPRINTS

For those who think they can sidestep pet waste ordinances, a company called PooPrints can catch the dog that did the dirty deed. PooPrints uses a dog's DNA to match a culprit to pet waste. Apartment buildings and condominiums where the program is used require residents to perform a simple cheek swab to collect and register their dogs' DNA. When property managers find pet waste that hasn't been picked up, they use a special collection kit to take a sample and send it for testing against the registry. The company matches the waste DNA against the registry and identifies the dog so the owner can be held accountable.

environmental pollutant that can carry bacteria, viruses, and parasites. Pet waste laws help keep communities sanitary and help prevent the spread of disease from dog to dog or from dog to human. The penalty for violating a pet waste ordinance varies by town, but it often involves a fine.

In McCandless, a suburb of Pittsburgh, Pennsylvania, a dog that defecates outside its yard can be declared a nuisance. Owners can be fined $50 for the first offense and up to $500 for the sixth offense.[1] In Springfield, Missouri, a city ordinance requires owners to pick up pet waste in most cases. "Many people don't realize that what their dog is leaving behind is essentially raw sewage. Pet waste is not part of the natural ecosystem and actually contains pollutants that are harmful to our waterways. It's not fertilizer. It's not compostable. It belongs in the trash," says Carrie Lamb, a water quality compliance officer in Springfield.[2]

LICENSES AND LIMITS

Almost all US cities and counties require dog owners to buy a dog license. Some licenses must be renewed annually, while others are lifetime licenses. A license tag should be attached to the dog's collar. If the dog is lost, the tag helps animal control officers identify the dog and return it to its home.

Local governments issue dog licenses. The fee varies by location and the type of dog. Dogs that are spayed or neutered or that have an elderly or low-income owner may qualify for a reduced license fee. Some dogs, such as service dogs, may be licensed at no cost.

The owner can be penalized with a fine if their unlicensed dog is caught. For example, in Pennsylvania, owners can be fined up to $300 plus court costs for not licensing a dog.[3] And if an animal control officer catches a lost dog that isn't licensed by an owner, the dog risks being euthanized before its family can be located.

IMPOUNDING LAWS

When a dog is found running loose, local laws allow animal control officers to impound it. Typically, they bring the dog to a local dog pound or animal shelter, where it is held for five to seven days, and notify its owner if possible. However, if a dog does not have tags or another form of identification, it may be challenging to find its owner. If the owner does not pick up the dog within the holding period, the dog may be placed for adoption or euthanized.

DOGS IN GERMANY

In Germany, people love their dogs. Dogs have been an important part of German families and society for centuries. Dogs are permitted almost everywhere with their owners. They ride the subway, go into stores, and are even allowed in many restaurants. Germans expect dogs in public to be well behaved, and a stranger may comment on a dog's behavior if it is not.

In Germany, numerous national and state laws apply to dogs and their owners. All dog owners must pay an annual tax and insurance fees on each dog they own. Each dog must also be microchipped. Spaying or neutering a dog is also required unless the owner is a breeder. All dogs must be leashed in public unless the owner and dog have attended dog training school and earned a dog handler's certificate and a green tag for the

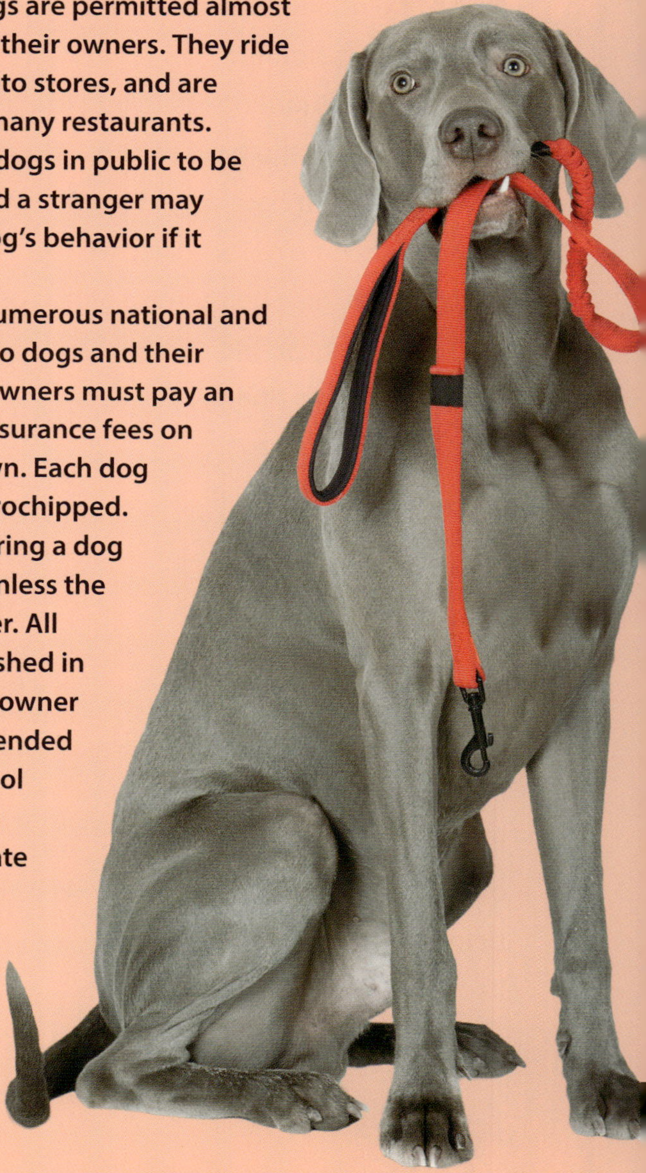

In Germany, off-leash dogs must be leashed when other people are near.

dog's collar. Fines for violating dog laws in Germany can be expensive. For example, a fine for not picking up waste can be up to 5,000 euros ($4,940 US dollars).[4]

There are also stringent regulations covering dogs' training and care. For example, some regulations forbid dogs from spending more than five hours in a crate at a time, while others ban using electric and prong collars. In 2020, Agricultural Minister Julia Klöckner proposed a new law that would require dog owners to have their dogs walked at least twice per day for a total walk time of one hour.[5]

Many jurisdictions also limit the number of dogs living in a single household. While rural locations may not restrict how many dogs an owner can have, cities generally have ordinances to limit dog ownership. The limit is typically two to four dogs per household. While not every town has a limit on dog ownership, many housing communities have their own rules. And in communities where there are no ownership limits, neighbors can file nuisance complaints if a neighbor's dogs are causing noise, odor, or unsanitary conditions.

LEASH LAWS

Some communities have passed laws requiring pet owners to keep their dogs on leashes in public spaces. These laws aim to protect both citizens and dogs. While the laws vary by community, they generally require a dog to be on a leash and under control anytime it is not on its property or in a designated off-leash area such as a dog park. For example, in South Carolina dogs are not permitted to run at large and must be leashed at all times in state parks.

Owners who violate leash laws can receive a ticket and a fine. In Tennessee, the leash law requires a dog to be under its owner's control. Dogs cannot run at large except when hunting or herding. If a dog is caught running at large, it can be impounded and placed in a shelter for at least five days. The owner must pay an impound fee to get the dog returned.

DOG BITE STATUTES

Sometimes dog bite injuries occur. Several states have dog bite statutes that hold dog owners liable for any injury caused when their dog bites another person. These laws vary from state to state. In Colorado, the dog bite statute applies only to a bite that causes severe injury. In Maine and Tennessee, the dog bite statute applies only when

Dogs that have bitten may be required to wear a muzzle, but dogs also wear muzzles for many other reasons. It's important to make sure a muzzle gives a dog enough room to pant so the dog doesn't overheat.

the bite occurs off the owner's property, while in Alabama, the statute applies only to bites on the owner's property. In many cases, a dog bite statute does not apply if the bitten person provoked the dog or if the person was in a place they were not allowed to be. Some dog bite statutes cover other injuries caused by a dog besides biting.

BREED-SPECIFIC LAWS

Some communities have passed breed-specific legislation (BSL) to regulate or ban certain dog breeds to decrease severe dog attacks. Breeds typically targeted by BSL are pit bull–type dogs, along with American bulldogs, Rottweilers, mastiffs, Dalmatians, Chow Chows, German shepherds, Doberman pinschers, and any mix of these breeds. BSL can include complete bans or mandatory sterilization, muzzling, microchipping, and fencing requirements. Many people consider BSL to be discriminatory and ineffective. Some states prohibit BSL and have passed laws to track and regulate dangerous dogs individually, regardless of breed.

Some states primarily use the one-bite rule to determine liability when a dog injures another person. This rule is named because it says that the dog can bite once, and after that, the owner knows it is dangerous and is liable for any future injuries. However, if the injured person provoked the dog or knowingly risked being bitten, the owner may not be liable for any injuries. The injuries are not limited to dog bites but can include other injuries caused by a dog.

BARKING AND NUISANCE LAWS

Many people have experienced a neighborhood dog barking for hours at a time. Some communities have a specific law or ordinance that targets barking dogs, and some have noise ordinances that apply. How much barking is considered a nuisance varies from place to place. However, dogs barking during the night or early morning or dogs that are excessively loud are typically considered a nuisance. The owner may be warned or fined when a dog's barking violates nuisance laws.

In Mount Lebanon, Pennsylvania, a local ordinance prohibits dogs from barking, yelping, or howling for 15 minutes or longer. "One of the most common dog complaints is about barking. Usually a warning and education rectifies the situation," said Laura Pace Lilley, a public information officer.[6] On the first violation, the owner may receive a warning. If the barking continues, the police can issue a citation and fine. There is an exception for dogs that bark when someone trespasses on their property.

Laws and regulations vary by community and state. Dog owners must be aware of the laws and ordinances where they live. If owners are unsure of their legal responsibilities, they can contact their local government for more information.

CHAPTER SEVEN

DOG DEBATES

For many people, dogs make fabulous pets. However, not everyone agrees on the best way to get a dog or how to care for it once it arrives home. Controversies have arisen over breeding and adoption, puppy mills, cropping and docking, training methods, and more. These controversies have sparked debate among dog lovers and the general public.

BREEDING VERSUS ADOPTION

One of the biggest debates surrounding dogs occurs before a dog even steps through the door of its new home. People should consider whether they should buy a dog from a breeder or adopt a dog from a rescue or shelter.

Some people prefer to buy a dog from a breeder. They may be looking for a purebred dog or need the dog to have specific qualities, such as a hypoallergenic coat. They may also want to bring a puppy home so

Some states have made it illegal for pet stores to sell puppies from commercial breeders.

they can shape the dog's training and socialization from a young age.

Not every breeder runs a responsible operation. Some are more concerned with profits than the welfare of the dogs. Dogs sold by pet stores, online sellers, or local flea markets are often from puppy mills. Puppy mills are commercial breeding facilities that sell as many puppies as possible for the highest profit. The dogs kept at these facilities often endure poor conditions and little medical care.

As a result, the puppies are often sick and have behavior issues. The breeding females may be kept in cages and bred repeatedly for years with little human contact and socialization. After the adult dogs can no longer produce litters, the puppy mills typically abandon them or sell them at auction. Often, the people who buy puppies from puppy mills are unaware of the conditions and treatment of the dogs at these facilities.

People who want to buy a puppy from a breeder should also be careful of smaller backyard breeders. A backyard breeder often does not have the knowledge or experience to be a responsible dog breeder. Backyard breeders may breed their pets with little knowledge about how to breed for health and temperament. They may not have information about the dogs' family history. Sometimes the dog becomes pregnant accidentally, and the owner decides to sell the puppies.

Backyard breeders often do not know how to ensure puppies are the healthiest they can be or screen the parents for genetic issues. They may also not know how to socialize a litter to give puppies a good start in life, and they may not be able to help the owners continue to raise the puppies. Puppies from backyard breeders might be less expensive than those from responsible breeders, but they may experience more health problems in the long run. Backyard breeders often ask customers few questions when they sell their puppies.

A responsible breeder's goal is to produce healthy dogs with good temperaments. They specialize in the care, grooming, and socialization of the dogs they breed, which takes a lot of time and effort. They often have a waiting list of potential families for available puppies. Responsible breeders carefully choose the dogs to breed and consider the parents' temperaments before breeding. They also perform genetic health testing on parents to

EARLY SEPARATION

Early separation is a red flag of an unreputable breeder. Puppies should never be separated from their mother or littermates before they reach eight weeks old. During the first eight weeks of life, a puppy learns critical social skills from its mother and littermates. If a puppy is separated too early, it will not learn these skills, leading to future behavior problems. A responsible breeder will not let a puppy leave its mother before it is eight weeks old, and many will have the puppies remain with their mothers for ten or 12 weeks.[1]

Responsible breeders regularly clean their puppies' living area.

screen them for genetic conditions and will provide this information to potential buyers.

When they look for breed-specific health issues, reputable breeders will screen both parents, performing tests such as hip X-ray certifications, canine eye exams, and heart defect testing. People breeding mixed-breed dogs will screen for the conditions of all the involved breeds. A responsible breeder will keep the puppies for as long as it takes to find them homes so they won't be dumped at a shelter. These breeders will also take back dogs they bred at any point if their owners can no longer care for them for any reason. They want to make sure their dogs don't add to the homeless pet problem.

Responsible breeders also want to ensure that their puppies will go to good homes where they fit in well with a family. These breeders carefully evaluate each potential buyer of a puppy. They ask potential owners many questions about their family and home environment. This information can help the breeder determine if the buyer's home and lifestyle meet a puppy's needs. Responsible breeders will also get to know their puppies' personalities and match them to prospective families. Often, they invite buyers to meet the puppy's parents, which can help buyers visualize the adult size and temperament of the puppy. If the father dog is not on-site, they can provide pictures and details about the dog.

THE CASE FOR ADOPTION

Other people strongly support adoption from a rescue or shelter. Adopting a dog from a shelter or rescue gives a deserving animal a good home and can save it from being euthanized. It also frees up shelter space or rescue resources to help other dogs in need. Adoption supporters also argue that adopting shelter dogs and not buying a dog from a puppy mill can fight the mills where it hurts the most: in the wallet. Elizabeth Oreck of Best Friends Animal Society says:

> *Each year, approximately 10,000 puppy mills across the country produce hundreds of thousands of dogs to be sold online and in pet stores throughout the nation. Meanwhile, approximately 3 to 4 million animals are killed in animal shelters annually as a means of population control. It's a sad illustration of the concept of supply and demand. If people would stop buying pets produced in puppy mills, and start adopting from shelters, we could put this industry out of business—and save every last homeless dog.*[2]

However, adopting a dog isn't always easy. The demand to adopt dogs from shelters and rescues is high in many parts of the country. And because so many dogs are now spayed or neutered, a lot of states need to bring in dogs from parts of the country with crowded shelters. Often, the dogs that are more easily adoptable are the ones transported. The people in regions with crowded shelters are left with dogs that may not work well in their homes.

Transportation also puts dogs at risk of stress, heat stroke, or escaping during transport. Additionally, only 5 percent of shelter dogs are purebred.[3] This means people may not find the type of dog they are seeking. Some rescues also have very strict home requirements, such as requiring a fenced yard or someone working

A responsible breeder introduces their puppies to a lot of sights, sounds, and objects to build the puppies' confidence.

from home, and some won't make any exceptions to these requirements.

Some dog rescue practices are also controversial. A few rescues have imported dogs from other countries and have unknowingly brought new strains of diseases with them. For example, a Canadian rescue group rescued a young dog from a Korean meat farm and brought it to western Canada in 2018. When the dog arrived in

Many people find it rewarding knowing that they gave a loving home to a dog that didn't have one.

Canada, it developed a cough and seizures and had to be euthanized. Scientists discovered that the dog carried a variant of the canine distemper virus that was common in Asia but never reported in North America.

Dr. Edward Dubovi, the director of the virology lab at the Animal Health Diagnostic Center at Cornell University, explained that this case highlights a larger problem. Rescue organizations may have good intentions but are not always educated on the viruses and illnesses foreign dogs can carry. "Well-meaning people are trying to save animals, but when you move animals, you move their infectious disease. If this particular Asia-1 strain got out into the wildlife population, then it's here forever, because you can't get rid of it once it hits wildlife," Dubovi wrote.[4]

In addition, some rescues and shelters have come under scrutiny for not being transparent about the dogs they are selling. They may label dogs that look like types that people are less interested in adopting, such as pit bulls, as another breed that more people want to adopt. A few have even adopted out dogs with known bite histories without telling the adoptive families. Some rescues also end up hoarding dogs. They take in more than they can care for.

Sometimes these rescues and shelters have good intentions. As dog lovers, they want every dog to have a loving family. They want every dog to be saved. The Animal Rescue Professionals Association has tips for potential owners to help them identify a responsible rescue. A good rescue or shelter should make sure the animals are up to date on veterinary care, provide adopters with health records, test the temperament of each dog, prioritize rescuing animals from its own state first, and be recommended by at least two nonprofit shelters in its state.

CROPPING AND DOCKING

Some controversies relate to surgical alterations of dogs. Ear cropping and tail docking are elective surgical

procedures frequently performed on some breeds, such as Dobermans, German shorthaired pointers, and schnauzers. The tail docking procedure removes part or all of a dog's tail when a puppy is only a few days old. "Docking's usually performed by a veterinarian or breeder without anesthesia, the rationale being that although it certainly causes pain, the puppy isn't fully alert yet and won't remember it," says Emily Patterson-Kane, an animal welfare scientist at the AVMA. Ear cropping involves cutting off part of a dog's ear leather so that it will stand upright rather than flop. This procedure is usually performed with anesthesia between six and 12 weeks of age.[5] The ears are taped to a hard surface while they heal to remain upright. It takes four to eight weeks for the ears to permanently stand up.

However, opposition to cropping and docking has grown. Critics say unnecessary procedures can lead to infection, complications, and pain, especially when they are performed without anesthesia. Several countries, including the United Kingdom and Australia, have largely banned ear cropping and tail docking, deeming it animal cruelty to perform unnecessary surgery on a dog. In other

The German pinscher is sometimes cropped and docked, *top*, but some people choose to leave the ears and tail natural, *bottom*.

DOG HAIR DYE

In December 2021, dog groomer Gabriel Feitosa appeared on television with a bichon frise. The white dog was dyed green to look like the holiday character the Grinch. Feitosa explained that he uses nontoxic and vegan hair dyes specially designed for dogs. However, the appearance sparked a debate over the ethics of dyeing pets' hair. Some people believe that as long as safe products designed for dogs are used, the practice is harmless. Others, however, believe the cosmetic makeover is unnecessary and potentially harmful to dogs.

countries, such as Canada, only certain regions have banned the procedure.

In the United Kingdom, docking is allowed for some working breeds, such as spaniels and pointers. This is because full tails are more likely to be injured when hunting as the tails hit the underbrush. The AVMA also opposes the practice in the United States. "The most common reason for cropping and docking is to give a dog a certain look. That means it poses unnecessary risks," says Patterson-Kane.[6]

ELECTRONIC DOG COLLARS

In recent years, training with electronic collars (e-collars) has grown in popularity. These collars, sometimes called shock collars, emit an electric pulse usually described as a static shock to a dog's neck through two small prongs attached to the collar. A remote-control unit triggers the electronic pulse, which can be set at various levels depending on the dog's sensitivity.

Trainers and owners can use these collars to deliver an unpleasant sensation to interrupt a dog's behavior. The timing of the correction is essential so the dog learns to associate the pulse with the undesired behavior and changes its behavior. Many trainers agree that e-collars can be safe and effective training tools when used correctly.

However, when e-collars are not used appropriately, they can be ineffective and can confuse and frighten a dog. Jean Donaldson, a dog trainer, opposes the use of e-collars. When misused, these collars can trigger fear and anxiety in dogs. Sensitive dogs may develop behavioral problems. "You end up trading a nuisance behavior—barking—for fear and anxiety, which is much harder to deal with," says Donaldson.[7]

PRONG COLLARS

Prong collars, also called pinch collars, are a type of training tool intended for strong or aggressive dogs. This type of collar is made of metal links, which can be expanded or shortened by adding or removing links. Each link has a set of metal prongs that rest against the dog's neck. If the dog starts to pull on a leash, the tension in the leash pulls the collar tighter, and the prongs pinch the dog's neck. They release when the dog stops pulling. However, using these collars is controversial as they can cause pain, choking, and tissue damage if misused, particularly for small dogs.

SAFETY
PUPPY

CHAPTER 8

ENRICHING LIVES

Although there are controversies around dog ownership and care, there are also many benefits. Dogs enrich their owners' lives, from providing companionship to reducing stress. Some dogs are trained as therapy dogs and service dogs to provide assistance and support for many types of physical, mental, and emotional conditions. Having a dog around can be a great way to make life better.

SERVICE DOGS

Service dogs help people with all types of health conditions and disabilities. They are highly skilled and specially trained animals that perform essential tasks for their owners. According to the Americans with Disabilities Act (ADA), a service dog is individually trained to do work or perform tasks to benefit a person with a disability. The person's disability could be

Service dogs go through extensive training before they officially start working.

physical, sensory, developmental, intellectual, psychiatric, or another type of disability. Service dogs have the right to go with their handlers in most public places.

Service dogs are not pets; they are working animals. The work they do must relate directly to their owner's disability. Service dogs' work includes guiding the blind, alerting deaf people to noises, alerting and protecting people with seizure disorders, pulling wheelchairs, calming people with psychiatric disorders, and more. Service dogs can go places where other animals are not allowed, including restaurants, public transportation, and libraries.

All service dogs must undergo extensive training to become certified service animals. Not every dog is suited to become a service animal; many dogs are easily

TRAINING WITH POSITIVE REINFORCEMENT

In recent years, science has shown the effectiveness of positive reinforcement in dog training. Positive reinforcement involves rewarding a dog for doing something right. A reward can be a treat, a toy, a game, attention, or anything the dog wants. By giving the dog something positive (a reward), it will perform the desired behavior more often in the future. And by focusing on rewards, the dog will learn to love training and not fear doing the wrong thing. It will try new things and attempt to earn rewards. The dog will associate the trainer with rewards, strengthening their bond.

distracted, aggressive, or uncomfortable around strangers. Therefore, trainers must first evaluate a potential service dog's temperament to determine whether the dog is an excellent candidate to become a service dog.

SNIFFING OUT CANCER

Dogs have a powerful sense of smell, and some use their noses to sniff out diseases such as cancer. Cancerous cells produce a specific odor, and dogs can detect it much earlier than human diagnostics can, even when cancer has not yet spread from its initial site. Dogs can even detect cancer's scent on a person's breath. Cancer-detecting dogs train for months by smelling samples of breath, saliva, plasma, and urine collected by doctors. After smelling hundreds of samples, the dogs learn to tell the difference between a cancerous sample and a healthy sample.

Dogs that make the best service animals often share several characteristics. First, good service dogs have a calm temperament, are eager to please, and enjoy being around people. They can focus on a task and ignore the many distractions they encounter in public. Intelligence is another desired quality because service dogs perform complex tasks for their owners. The dogs must also be comfortable around other people and animals.

Some dog breeds are better suited as service dogs than others. The four most common breeds are sometimes called the Fab Four. These are the Labrador

LABRADOR RETRIEVER

The Labrador retriever was the most popular breed in the United States for 31 years in a row, holding that position through 2021.[1] The Lab is a medium- to large-sized dog. The Lab stands from 21.5 to 24.5 inches (54.6–62.2 cm) at the shoulder. The breed weighs between 55 and 80 pounds (25–36 kg).[2]

The Lab is often used to retrieve waterfowl. Its thick, water-repellent coat sheds a lot and comes in three colors: yellow, black, and chocolate. It has a broad head and a thick tail called an otter tail that helps the dog turn in the water.

Labrador retrievers are known for their friendly, outgoing personalities. They are very affectionate and can make good family dogs. Labs also socialize well with other dogs and humans.

These dogs are athletic with lots of energy. As a result, they need a lot of exercise to stay physically and mentally fit. Because of their physical strength, easygoing personality, and intelligence, Labrador retrievers make excellent service and therapy dogs.

retriever, golden retriever, standard poodle, and collie. Other breeds, including the Bernese mountain dog, Border collie, boxer, German shepherd, Great Dane, Pomeranian, miniature and toy poodle, and Portuguese water dog, also have success as service dogs.

THERAPY DOGS

Some dogs work as therapy dogs and visit hospitals, schools, and nursing homes. These dogs provide comfort. Research shows that therapy dogs can improve a patient's mood and reduce pain and stress levels. Children often respond well to therapy dogs. When a therapy dog is present, children are more likely to participate in treatments and remain calm. Therapy dogs promote social interaction for all ages and reduce stress, anxiety, and loneliness.

Dogs that make good therapy dogs must be gentle with strangers and good at meeting new people. With training, the dog must work well in busy environments with many distractions. It should be calm and trained not to jump, lick, or invade personal space. While individuals of any breed or mix can be good therapy dogs, some breeds are more naturally suited to the work. These include golden retrievers, Labrador retrievers, standard poodles, Yorkshire terriers, pugs, Great Danes, and Newfoundlands.

EMOTIONAL SUPPORT DOGS

Emotional support dogs provide comfort and companionship to people with mental health conditions. The presence of emotional support dogs helps relieve the symptoms of their owners' mental health conditions. People with a qualifying mental health condition can get a letter from a licensed mental health professional with a prescription or recommendation to register their dog as an emotional support animal. An emotional support dog can live in housing that doesn't normally allow dogs. But emotional support dogs are not service animals under the ADA since they do not perform specific tasks for a person with a disability, so they cannot go to public places that do not allow pet dogs.

Cooper is a Shih Tzu that works as a therapy dog at Harvard Medical School's Countway Library. Cooper arrives at the library twice a week and heads to his office. There he is ready to play, snuggle, or sit quietly with those who come to see him.

"Ever since he was young, we realized that Cooper has a very calm demeanor and he is sensitive to people's emotions," says Dr. Loise Francisco, a researcher at Harvard Medical School who adopted Cooper. Cooper helps students, staff, and faculty who need a little stress relief during the day, spending up to 30 minutes with them. Librarian Wendy Brown says that there are fewer complaints on days when Cooper is working: "Just this morning, we had someone come by and say, 'I don't know what it is, but he just makes me happy.'"[3]

Some therapy dogs visit hospital patients. Therapy dog teams typically consist of a volunteer owner and their dog.

HEALTH BENEFITS OF DOGS

People who own dogs may experience several health benefits. A 2019 analysis found that people who own a dog are less likely to die of any cause than people without a dog. Dog ownership was even more strongly linked to better health outcomes for a person who had already had a heart attack or stroke. These owners were 31 percent less likely to die from cardiovascular disease than other people without a dog who had a heart attack or stroke.[4]

A separate study from Sweden in 2019 had similar results. People who lived with a dog better recovered

Because many dogs are energetic and all need to be taken outside regularly, dogs can give people a reason to exercise more, which helps owners stay healthier.

from heart attacks and strokes than people without a dog. The health benefits were most significant for dog owners who lived alone. Dr. Haider Warraich, director of the heart failure program at the VA Boston Healthcare System, says, "These studies suggest that adopting a dog may be as much of a service to your own health as the dog's."[5]

Some of the health benefits of dogs can be attributed to increased activity and exercise. People with dogs typically get outside to exercise more often than people who do not have a dog. Regular walking and playing with a dog can have several health benefits, such as decreasing blood pressure, cholesterol levels, and triglyceride levels. People who walk their dogs regularly also reduce their risk of diabetes.

Dogs also provide social and emotional support for their families. Dogs serve as companions, reducing loneliness and depression for their owners. Research shows that simply petting a dog can reduce levels of cortisol, a stress hormone. Also, the interaction between a person and a dog can increase levels of oxytocin, a hormone that creates good feelings.

For Robert Doward, his dog Maria provided much-needed support when he struggled with anxiety and depression. He had been working more hours than

Play helps improve both the owner's mood and the dog's.

usual at his job when his mental health plummeted, and he became overwhelmed. One day, he started crying and couldn't stop. With therapy, a new job, and changes in his personal life, Doward's mental health slowly improved. However, he says his dog was an essential part of his recovery. "Taking her out for walks, getting out into fresh air, just putting one foot in front of the other, that lifts your spirits. And then there's nothing like having a dog curled up beside you, even when you feel absolutely miserable. She'll check my face anxiously, as if she knows something

Food puzzles sometimes require a dog to slide knobs or lift up pieces to expose hidden treats.

is wrong. And that makes me smile—and that somehow makes you feel better. There is just something magic about dogs. Honestly, she got me through," says Doward.[6]

IMPROVING CARE

More owners are thanking their dogs by improving their care. People have become more aware of the importance of letting dogs stop and sniff on walks. They are learning the importance of letting their dogs use their brains, such as by feeding some meals in food puzzles.

Owners are also learning about the importance of giving their pets choices when possible. Having choices helps dogs feel safe by giving them some control of their lives. Choices can be to refuse to be petted or hugged, to go to a safe spot and not be bothered, and to decide whether to participate in a training or grooming session.

For thousands of years, dogs have stood by their human partners with their loyal and protective nature. Today, dogs remain one of the most popular and common pets worldwide. These four-legged friends provide companionship to many people and use their skills to help others. For many people, life would not be the same without a dog.

OWNING A DOG

Dogs were the first species to be domesticated. They are social animals that do well living alongside people. They have been bred for centuries to help people with various tasks.

DIET: Dogs are carnivores. Whatever food owners decide to feed their dogs, they should ensure it is nutritionally complete by checking that it is formulated to match widely accepted standards or working with a canine nutritionist.

SPACE: Most dogs do best living in the home with their owners. They need daily exercise in the form of walking, running, and playing.

ROUTINE CARE: An annual visit to the veterinarian is essential for keeping a dog healthy and detecting potential health problems before they become significant. All dogs need regular grooming, including brushing and nail trimming.

ENRICHMENT: Dogs are smart and need to regularly engage their minds. Food puzzles, training, and sniffing on walks are some of the ways to provide dogs with enrichment.

KEY BREEDS

- The Chihuahua is a small dog that originated in Mexico. It can have short or long hair, and it has large eyes.
- The dachshund is a German breed with short legs, a long body, long ears, and a coat that is usually tan or black and tan.
- The German shepherd is a large, agile, muscular dog. It is smart and often used as a police or military dog.
- The golden retriever is a sturdy, muscular, medium-sized dog with a gentle, friendly nature and a golden coat.
- The Havanese is a small, friendly dog native to Cuba. It has a silky coat that comes in a variety of colors.
- The Irish wolfhound is the tallest dog breed recognized by the American Kennel Club.
- The Labrador retriever is a medium- to large-sized dog with a friendly, outgoing personality. With their easygoing nature and intelligence, Labrador retrievers make excellent service and therapy dogs.
- The mastiff is a massive and strong dog that can weigh more than an adult human and is loyal and protective of its family.
- The poodle is a highly intelligent and athletic breed with thick, curly hair. Because it comes in three sizes (toy, miniature, and standard), does not shed much, and is hypoallergenic, the breed is popular with many households.

GLOSSARY

DNA
Deoxyribonucleic acid, the chemical that is the basis of genetics, through which various traits are passed from parent to child.

docile
Easily managed.

enrichment
The act or process of making life richer by adding or increasing desirable things.

genetic
Having to do with genes, which are in DNA and control different traits.

hypoallergenic
Less likely to produce an allergic reaction.

larva
The immature form of an animal that grows and changes its body form through metamorphosis.

liable
To be bound or responsible according to law.

neuter
To remove the reproductive organs of an animal, especially a male.

ordinance
A law or statute.

parasite
An organism that lives on or in a host organism and gets its food from or at the expense of its host.

plasma
The clear, yellow liquid part of the blood.

registry
An organization that keeps an official record book that lists individuals of a breed and their family trees.

socialization
The process of preparing a dog to become comfortable in the presence of other animals and people and to experience a variety of places, sights, sounds, and more.

spay
To remove the reproductive organs of a female animal.

temperament
An animal's nature and how it affects its behavior.

ADDITIONAL RESOURCES

SELECTED BIBLIOGRAPHY

"Domestic Dog." *National Geographic*, n.d., nationalgeographic.com. Accessed 13 Oct. 2022.

"How Shifting Supply and Demand Could End Puppy Mills and Shelter Killing." *Columbus Dispatch*, 10 May 2016, dispatch.com. Accessed 13 Oct. 2022.

"The Responsible Pet Owner's Checklist for Taking Care of a Pet." *PetMD*, 19 Mar. 2019, petmd.com. Accessed 13 Oct. 2022.

FURTHER READINGS

The Complete Dog Breed Book. DK, 2020.

Frydenborg, Kay. *A Dog in the Cave: The Wolves Who Made Us Human*. Houghton Mifflin Harcourt, 2017.

Pearson, Marie. *Essential Mammals*. Abdo, 2022.

ONLINE RESOURCES

Booklinks
NONFICTION NETWORK
FREE! ONLINE NONFICTION RESOURCES

To learn more about dogs, please visit **abdobooklinks.com** or scan this QR code. These links are routinely monitored and updated to provide the most current information available.

MORE INFORMATION

For more information on this subject, contact or visit the following organizations:

Alliance of Therapy Dogs

1919 Morrie Ave.
Cheyenne, WY 82001
office@therapydogs.com
therapydogs.com

The Alliance of Therapy Dogs is a national organization that provides certification, registration, and support for members and their therapy dogs.

American Kennel Club (AKC)

101 Park Ave., 5th floor
New York, NY 10178
akc.org

The AKC is a registry of purebred dogs in the United States. In addition to maintaining its pedigree registry, the AKC also promotes and sanctions events for purebred dogs.

Association of Professional Dog Trainers

2365 Harrodsburg Rd., A325
Lexington, KY 40504
membership@apdt.com
apdt.com

The Association of Professional Dog Trainers is an organization that offers membership to dog trainers and holds them to a code of ethics. It also provides education to the public about dog training and holds training conferences.

SOURCE NOTES

CHAPTER 1. OUR BEST FRIEND

1. "How Powerful Is a Dog's Nose?" *Phoenix Veterinary Center*, n.d., phoenixvetcenter.com. Accessed 17 Feb. 2023.

2. "Facts + Statistics: Pet Ownership and Insurance." *Insurance Information Institute*, n.d., iii.org. Accessed 17 Feb. 2023.

3. "Mastiff." *American Kennel Club*, n.d., akc.org. Accessed 17 Feb. 2023.

4. "Irish Wolfhound." *American Kennel Club*, n.d., akc.org. Accessed 17 Feb. 2023.

5. "Chihuahua." *American Kennel Club*, n.d., akc.org. Accessed 17 Feb. 2023.

CHAPTER 2. NATURAL HISTORY OF DOGS

1. Helen Briggs. "How Did Dogs Become Our Best Friends? New Evidence." *BBC News*, 19 July 2017, bbc.com. Accessed 17 Feb. 2023.

2. Mary Bates. "Prehistoric Puppy May Be Earliest Evidence of Pet-Human Bonding." *National Geographic*, 27 Feb. 2018, nationalgeographic.com. Accessed 17 Feb. 2023.

3. Briggs, "How Did Dogs Become Our Best Friends?"

4. "Frequently Asked Questions." *Saint Bernard Club of America*, n.d., saintbernardclubofamerica.club. Accessed 17 Feb. 2023.

5. "Presentation of Our Organisation." *Fédération Cynologique Internationale*, n.d., fci.be. Accessed 17 Feb. 2023.

CHAPTER 3. GETTING A NEW DOG

1. Kimberly Alt. "Dog Life Expectancy Chart: How Long Do Dogs Live?" *Canine Journal*, 29 Nov. 2022, caninejournal.com. Accessed 17 Feb. 2023.

2. Nicole Spector. "Adopting a Pet? Ask Yourself These Questions First." *Better by Today*, 12 Sept. 2019, nbcnews.com. Accessed 17 Feb. 2023.

3. Krista Mifflin. "The Price of a Purebred Puppy: You Should Get What You Pay For." *Spruce Pets*, 13 Jan. 2020, thesprucepets.com. Accessed 17 Feb. 2023.

4. Sassafras Lowrey. "Before You Adopt: Planning a Lifelong Commitment to Your Pet's Health." *New York Times*, 31 Mar. 2020, nytimes.com. Accessed 17 Feb. 2023.

5. "Female Canine Urinary Incontinence." *Merck Animal Health*, n.d., merck-animal-health-usa.com. Accessed 17 Feb. 2023.

CHAPTER 4. TAKING CARE OF A DOG

1. "General Dog Care." *American Society for the Prevention of Cruelty to Animals*, n.d., aspca.org. Accessed 17 Feb. 2023.

2. "The Responsible Pet Owner's Checklist for Taking Care of a Pet." *PetMD*, 19 Mar. 2019, petmd.com. Accessed 17 Feb. 2023.

3. "Responsible Pet Owner's Checklist."

4. "Responsible Pet Owner's Checklist."

5. "Responsible Pet Owner's Checklist."

6. Karolina Brunius Enlund, et al. "Dog Owners' Perspectives on Canine Dental Health—A Questionnaire Study in Sweden." *Frontiers in Veterinary Science*, vol. 7, 2020, p. 298, ncbi.nlm.nih.gov. Accessed 17 Feb. 2023.

7. "Responsible Pet Owner's Checklist."

CHAPTER 5. INDUSTRY AND COMMUNITY

1. Sally Jones. "The True Cost of Owning a Dog: Can You Really Afford That Furry Friend?" *Canine Journal*, 13 Jan. 2023, caninejournal.com. Accessed 17 Feb. 2023.

2. James Rhys Clarke. "15 Biggest Dog Companies in the World and Their Most Popular Brands." *Top Dog Tips*, 31 Nov. 2021, topdogtips.com. Accessed 17 Feb. 2023.

3. Emma Bedford. "Pet Industry Expenditure in the United States from 1994 to 2021 (in Billion US Dollars)." *Statista*, 13 May 2022, statista.com. Accessed 17 Feb. 2023.

4. Emma Bedford. "Market Share of the Leading Pet Store Companies in the United States in 2022, Based on Revenue." *Statista*, 13 Oct. 2022, statista.com. Accessed 17 Feb. 2023.

5. "About the American Kennel Club." *American Kennel Club*, n.d., akc.org. Accessed 17 Feb. 2023.

6. Sassafras Lowrey. "Dog Owners: Breed Clubs Need You!" *American Kennel Club*, 17 Dec. 2019, akc.org. Accessed 17 Feb. 2023.

7. Abbey Marshall. "Holy Poodle, Batman! Akron Therapy Dog's Superhero Routine Wins National Trick Competition." *Akron Beacon Journal*, 12 Jan. 2022, beaconjournal.com. Accessed 17 Feb. 2023.

8. "The State of Animal Welfare Today." *Best Friends Animal Society*, n.d., bestfriends.org. Accessed 17 Feb. 2023.

CHAPTER 6. LAWS AND REGULATIONS

1. Linda Wilson Fuoco. "Towns Have Tougher Dog Laws to Put a Leash on Nuisance." *Pittsburgh Post-Gazette*, 31 Oct. 2019, post-gazette.com. Accessed 17 Feb. 2023.

2. "Poo Disposal." *City of Springfield*, n.d., springfieldmo.gov. Accessed 17 Feb. 2023.

3. "License Your Dog in PA." *Pennsylvania Department of Agriculture*, n.d., licenseyourdogpa.pa.gov. Accessed 17 Feb. 2023.

4. James Oliver. "12 Interesting Dog Laws in Germany to Know." *Via Travelers*, 3 Feb. 2023, viatravelers.com. Accessed 17 Feb. 2023.

5. Lito Howse and Sheena Goodyear. "Germany Wants to Make People Walk Their Dogs for 1 Hour a Day—But Not Everyone Can." *CBC*, 19 Aug. 2020, cbc.ca. Accessed 17 Feb. 2023.

6. Wilson Fuoco, "Towns Have Tougher Dog Laws."

CHAPTER 7. DOG DEBATES

1. "How Responsible Breeders Differ from Puppy Mills, Pet Shops, Backyard Breeders." *Golden Meadows*, 11 Apr. 2018, goldenmeadowsretrievers.com. Accessed 17 Feb. 2023.

2. "How Shifting Supply and Demand Could End Puppy Mills and Shelter Killing." *Columbus Dispatch*, 10 May 2016, dispatch.com. Accessed 17 Feb. 2023.

3. Meilan Solly. "Genetic Testing Shows Animal Shelters Often Misidentify Dogs' Breeds." *Smithsonian Magazine*, 27 Aug. 2017, smithsonianmag.com. Accessed 17 Feb. 2023.

4. Michael Brice-Saddler. "Want to Rescue a Dog from Overseas? It Might Carry a New Strain of Disease, Researchers Say." *Washington Post*, 27 Mar. 2019, washingtonpost.com. Accessed 17 Feb. 2023.

5. Camille Noe Pagán. "Ear Cropping and Tail Docking: Should You or Shouldn't You?" *Fetch by WebMD*, 3 Feb. 2014, pets.webmd.com. Accessed 17 Feb. 2023.

6. Pagán, "Ear Cropping and Tail Docking."

7. Sadie Dingfelder. "You Can Shock Your Dog into Behaving. Should That Be Banned?" *Washington Post*, 7 Mar. 2016. washingtonpost.com. Accessed 17 Feb. 2023.

CHAPTER 8. ENRICHING LIVES

1. Natasha Dado. "Labrador Retriever Named Most Popular Dog Breed for 31 Consecutive Years: 'Record-Breaking Run.'" *People*, 15 Mar. 2022, people.com. Accessed 17 Feb. 2023.

2. "Labrador Retriever." *American Kennel Club*, n.d., akc.org. Accessed 17 Feb. 2023.

3. Christine Junge and Ann MacDonald. "Therapy Dog Offers Stress Relief at Work." *Harvard Health Publishing: Harvard Medical School*, 22 July 2011, health.harvard.edu. Accessed 17 Feb. 2023.

4. Sandee LaMotte. "Owning a Dog Tied to Lowering Your Risk of Dying Early by 24%, Says Science." *CNN Health*, 8 Oct. 2019, cnn.com. Accessed 17 Feb. 2023.

5. Linda Carroll. "Owning a Dog Linked to Lower Risk of Death after a Heart Attack, Study Finds." *NBC News*, 8 Oct. 2019, nbcnews.com. Accessed 17 Feb. 2023.

6. Ann Robinson. "'Dogs Have a Magic Effect': How Pets Can Improve Our Mental Health." *Guardian*, 17 Mar. 2020, theguardian.com. Accessed 17 Feb. 2023.

INDEX

ABOUT THE AUTHOR

Carla Mooney is a graduate of the University of Pennsylvania with a degree in economics. Today, she writes for young people and is the author of many books for young adults and children. Mooney enjoys taking walks and snuggling on the couch with her dog Lily, a mini goldendoodle.